Also by Eve Bunting

The Summer of Riley
Blackwater

SERIOUSLY
STINKY
TRAINERS

EVE BUNTING

An imprint of HarperCollinsPublishers

To my sons – who had a few pairs

First published in Great Britain by Collins in 2003
Collins is an imprint of HarperCollins*Publishers*
77 – 85 Fulham Palace Rd, London, W6 8JB
The HarperCollins website address is www.**fire**and**water**.co.uk

First published in the USA by HarperCollins Children's Books, a division of
HarperCollins*Publishers*, 10 East 43rd Street New York, NY 10022
as *Nasty Stinky Sneakers* in 1994.

ISBN 0 00 713002 3

Printed and bound in England by Clays Ltd, St Ives plc

one

Colin stopped outside the door of his flat. He took off his left trainer.

His friend Webster gasped, then grinned. "Superb," he said.

Colin unlaced the right trainer, "Wait till you get a whiff of this one. It's even better." He pulled it off and wafted it under Webster's nose.

Webster closed his eyes and sighed happily. "Ferocious!" he said. "There's no other guy in the world going to beat that. Not Jack Dunn, not anybody. Those have to be the stinkiest trainers in the world."

Colin had carefully placed them side by side and Webster touched one with his toe.

"But I'm still nervous about your leaving them outside the door."

"I have to," Colin said. "My mum won't let them in the flat till I'm absolutely, finally ready for bed."

"Even if you bag them?"

"Even if I triple-bag them and lock them in my wardrobe," Colin said. "And anyway, as my mum says, who'd want them? Who'd touch them? I'm having trouble myself." He pulled out the key that he kept on a cord around his neck.

Mr Sabaton and his bulldog, Bruno, came down the stairs from his upstairs flat. Bruno was on his lead. His little flat bulldog nose twitched. It found the floor and made a direct track towards the trainers.

"Hold, boy! Back!" Mr Sabaton ordered. He scowled at Colin. "Are those abominations yours?"

"A bomb what?" Colin asked.

"Those are trainers, Mr Sabaton," Webster explained. "They aren't Slam Dunkers, but when Colin wins the Stinkiest Trainers in the World contest he'll get three pairs of Slam Dunkers. They're the best."

Mr Sabaton's nose wrinkled. "Someone is vulgar enough to have a smelly-trainer contest?"

"Sure. It's up in Jamison Park. The people who make Slam Dunkers are running it. Slam Dunkers are probably so classy they never stink. I'm Colin's manager," Webster went on. "You know, his coach for the competition. Jack Dunn, he's in our class and he's a real jerk, he's trying, too. But his stinkies aren't in the same league. We think he cheats, too."

Bruno had managed to drag Mr Sabaton close to the trainers. But now, just a paw length away, he sat back on his hind legs and moaned.

Webster gazed at the dog in awe. "See that? Those trainers are so nasty even the dog's gagging."

Mr Sabaton pointed at Colin. "Young man, I need to speak to your mother. Your shoes are polluting the entire building. They can't be left out here."

"My mum's at work," Colin said.

"Your father then."

"He's sleeping," Colin said. "He works nights."

"You could speak to Amy," Webster said. "Colin's sister. But she's only seven. We're ten," he added helpfully. Webster was always helpful.

"Humph," Mr Sabaton said.

"Anyway," Colin told him, "tomorrow's the competition. It'll be over soon. I won't be leaving my new ones outside."

"Humph," Mr Sabaton said again.

Colin and Webster watched him stomp down the corridor between the flats. Bruno seemed to be in a hurry to get out into the fresh air.

"Who'd want them? Who'd take them?" Webster asked, imitating Colin. "That man for one. He'd dump them and then bingo. No prize. Remember, one pair of those Slam Dunkers belongs to me. My fee."

"I know. I know." Colin opened the flat door. "Mr Sabaton won't touch them. He keeps to himself, but he's an OK guy. My mum says his bark's worse than his bite."

"His bite's probably better than his wimpy dog's." Webster took one last look at the smelly, stinky trainers before he followed Colin into the flat.

two

Amy was building a tower of Lego blocks on the kitchen table. "Phe-ew," she said. "Colin! Your feet smell like dead skunks."

"Thanks. It's from my trainers." Colin lifted one bare foot and Amy cringed.

"Get that skunk away from me," she said.

"You won't be saying that when I win you a new pair of Slam Dunkers," Colin said.

"I know. I love them. But I don't have to love your stinky feet, do I?"

"Is Dad awake yet?" Colin asked.

Amy shook her head. "He got home really late. He left a note. He doesn't want to be woken up till four."

"Oh." Colin poured a glass of juice for Webster and one for himself. Dad seemed to be working harder and harder. And longer and longer. Mum, too. Sometimes Colin heard their whispered talk about bills and rent money. The talk stopped when he appeared. A pair of Slam Dunkers for Amy and a pair for him and a pair for Webbie, of course, that would save his mum and dad a lot of money. Slam Dunkers would probably last for ever, too.

Webster spread their game plan on the kitchen table beside Amy's tower.

"Careful," she warned. "Knock it over and you're dead."

Webster leaned over the paper. "Last day," he reminded Colin. "Is there anything else we could have done?" He nibbled on his pencil rubber, which was already chewed down to the rim.

"*No socks.*" He had ticked that. "You've done that."

"*Jogging to get your feet juicy.*" He'd ticked that, too.

"Yuck," Amy said without looking up.

"You won't be saying yuck—" Colin began.

"I know, I know. It's just... do we have to keep talking about sweat?"

"*No washing of feet,*" Webster continued.

"That part was hard," Colin said. "Showering with plastic bags taped over your feet is hazardous to your health. You slip and slide. Sometimes water leaks in, then your feet get funny-looking, like dead white fish."

Amy squinted her eyes and then put another Lego block on top of her tower. "One time he used Mum's shower cap," she told Webster. "He taped his feet together."

"I had to hop," Colin said. "Hop in the shower!"

"And when Mum went to use the cap she screamed – I mean screamed," Amy added.

"You mean it smelled bad, even after just one time?" Webster was really interested.

Amy rolled her eyes.

"I never used her shower cap again," Colin said.

Amy grinned. "Mum didn't either."

"Just a minute." Webster went to the door, opened it, came back, and said, "Still there."

Colin nodded. "They're safe. This isn't New York City, you know, Webbie. It's just a little town, and this is just a little block of flats."

"It used to be a house once," Amy volunteered.

"I know," Webster said.

"Ours and three other flats," Colin went on.

"OK, OK," Webster said. "I don't need its history. I was just checking." He consulted his list again. *"Sleeping with your trainers on."*

Colin nodded. "Every night. And I had to take my own sheets over to the Launderette. And use a separate machine. I'm so sick of that Launderette. A good thing it's just across the street and the video arcade's right next door."

Webster nibbled on the rubber and narrowed his eyes at Colin. "Are you absolutely sure you shouldn't go and tramp around under the oak tree in Jamison Park? Every dog in town visits that oak tree. All those fallen leaves like mulch. You'd never know what you were walking in."

"Oh, grosso!" Amy stood up so fast that the tower staggered, then righted itself.

"I seriously recommend the oak tree," Webster said, "as a finishing touch."

Colin shook his head. "Uh-uh. The rules say no out-of-the-ordinary stuff allowed, and that would be out of the ordinary. I'd never willingly go somewhere to walk in dog poop."

Amy put her hands over her ears. "I can't stand it. And I'm going to warn you about something else, Colin Kyle. I know you think Poppy Roginski is going to like you more when you win a smelly, stinky-trainer competition, but she's not. Girls go for rock stars, and baseball stars and—"

"I don't want Poppy Roginski to like me more," Colin said.

"Jack Dunn wants her to like him," Webster said. "I can't figure it out. Poppy Roginski has blue teeth. Why would anybody like a girl with blue teeth?"

"She does not have blue teeth," Colin said. "She wears blue-coloured braces on her teeth. They're cool. She has pink ones, too, for special occasions. Her friend Rachel told me."

"There you are," Amy hooted. "Colin loves Poppy Roginski. He loves her, and he partly wants to be the smelly, stinky-trainer king because of her."

"Shut up, Amy," Colin warned. "I never even talked to Poppy Roginski, not even once."

"But you wish you'd talked to her. You wish

you'd kissed her," Amy said, and moved quickly to put the table between them.

Webster stood up. "I think I have to go," he said. "See you, Colin. If you change your mind about Jamison Park..." He had the door open.

"Oh, no," he said. "Oh, no."

"What? What?" Colin and Amy were right behind him.

The smelly, stinky trainers were gone.

three

Colin, Webster and Amy stood staring at the empty spot by the door. A faint rotten smell hung in the air like a memory.

"It was that Mr Sabaton," Webster said. "He took the trainers."

"I bet it was Bruno," Colin said.

"You mean the dog took them in his *mouth*?" Amy asked. "There's no dog in the world would..." She stopped.

Mr Sabaton and Bruno, still on his lead, were coming in the front door.

Webster leaned forward, but Colin grabbed his arm.

They waited.

"Mr Sabaton, did you take my trainers?" Colin asked.

"The bomb ones," Webster added, helpful as ever.

"The abominations?" Mr Sabaton looked at the trainerless space. "Certainly not. I would not touch anything so vile."

Webster jerked a thumb at Bruno, who was sniffing in the direction of Colin's bare feet. "How about him?"

"My dog has better taste," Mr Sabaton said.

"Well, la-di-da. Excuse us—" Webster began, but Colin was watching Bruno.

"Hey," he said. "I have an idea. Mr Sabaton, maybe Bruno could lead us to the trainers. Maybe he could follow the scent."

"You call that stink a scent?" Mr Sabaton asked.

"Please, Mr Sabaton," Amy chimed in. "It's really important."

Mr Sabaton gave his little "humph". "Oh, very well," he said. "Bruno does have a little bloodhound in him. He will probably be an excellent tracker. Go to it, fellow. Follow the trail."

Colin held a foot under Bruno's little pushed-in nose and Bruno staggered back a couple of paces, then revived. He blinked, drooled, then began sniffing along the corridor, yelping happy little yelps.

Mr Sabaton held fast to the lead as he was pulled along.

Bruno pawed at the outside door.

Colin opened it for him.

"You know, there might be something in it for the dog who leads us to the trainers," Webster said. "Bone, Bruno. Steak. A nice piece of chicken gizzard."

"Please don't confuse him," Mr Sabaton ordered.

Bruno crossed the pavement and stopped at the kerb. A large bus with a Lion King ad on its side roared by. A supermarket truck rumbled past.

Bruno sat down and hung his head.

"What, boy? What? I don't understand. Here..." Colin held up one of his feet so that Bruno could have a reinforcing sniff.

"The trail may continue across the street," Mr Sabaton said. "But I neglected to tell you, Bruno is afraid of traffic. He will not cross the street. When we walk I have to plan our course very carefully." He made circles in the air with his hand. "Round and round and round. It gets a little boring."

"I think the trail does continue across the street," Colin said, "but what can we do?" He felt desperate. There had to be a way. He knew what it was.

"Mr Sabaton," Colin said, "could Webbie

and I carry Bruno across the street? We'd be really gentle, honest. Then he could pick up the trail on the other side."

"Please, Mr Sabaton." Amy closed her eyes and looked heavenward.

"The other side of the street could be very inspiring for Bruno," Webster said helpfully. "New places are, you know. It kind of peps you up. He might think he was in another world."

"Perhaps, perhaps." Mr Sabaton unsnapped the lead. "You may carry him. But careful as you go. Bruno has a delicate digestive system."

Webster grabbed Bruno's back legs. "I'll take this end in case he is sick."

"Thanks a lot," Colin said. "Amy, be ready to support the middle."

"On the crossing, please," Mr Sabaton directed. "Safety first."

He walked ahead of them, stopping traffic.

Colin and Webster heaved and panted. Bruno had gone as limp and heavy as a dead rhinoceros. His eyes were closed. His tongue lolled from his mouth like a pink Popsicle. His legs dangled.

Amy skipped between them, sidestepping, rubbing Bruno's stomach.

"Are you all right, Bruno?" she asked. "All right, doggie?"

Bruno whimpered an answer that none of them understood.

When they reached the other pavement, Mr Sabaton ordered, "Put him down. Tenderly now. Tenderly. This could be a severe shock to the system."

Colin and Webster straightened Bruno's legs and stood him up.

He collapsed on his belly.

"Look around you, Bruno. You'll be pepped up by the interesting new landscape," Webster advised.

Amy gently slapped Bruno's slack jowls. "Doggie? Doggie?"

Colin wiggled his toes under Bruno's nose and Bruno stiffened. His eyes opened.

"It's like a miracle," Amy said.

"My cat wakes up like that for fish," Webster said.

"Come on, Bruno. Come on, boy. Find the trainer thief," Colin urged.

"Be a hero," Webster added. "Be Rin Tin Tin. Lassie Come Home."

Bruno's ears went up. His tail thumped. He took one last look at them, then charged. Bruno was definitely on the scent.

four

Mr Sabaton snapped the lead into place.

Bruno snuffled along the pavement. His head was down, his bottom was up. His nose sniffed from side to side.

"He's being a vacuum cleaner." Webster made a quick grab for Bruno's tail.

"Don't mess with him," Colin said. "Let him concentrate."

"I was wondering if perhaps we should blindfold him," Mr Sabaton suggested. "Fewer distractions, you know."

"Great idea," Colin said. "But with what?"

Mr Sabaton pulled a red handkerchief from his pocket and tied it around Bruno's eyes. Bruno's tail never stopped wagging.

Then he was off again. He passed the doughnut shop.

"Remarkable," Mr Sabaton said.

"He's on to something better than doughnuts," Webster said.

Colin hopped on one foot. He picked a pebble of hard chewing gum off the sole of his other foot. Fortunately, it was not a stringy piece.

Bruno passed the TV repair shop. He passed the Chinese market. He passed the Launderette. He dragged Mr Sabaton into the video arcade with him.

Colin and Webster and Amy stopped. The place was almost empty, and not much wonder. It smelled terrible.

Jack Dunn and his friend Croak were playing a video game. They were wearing their football strips with the red windbreakers that said POWER-UP in big white letters across the back. Their boots hung on long laces over their shoulders. One glance told Colin that Jack Dunn had his own trainers on. Spaceman zoomed across a lighted screen in front of them.

Bruno pulled so hard on his lead that it slipped out of Mr Sabaton's hand. He bounded across the floor to grovel at Jack Dunn's feet.

"Oh, my gosh," Amy whispered. "How did he do that when he couldn't even see? But those aren't your trainers, are they, Colin?"

"Course not," Colin said. "Bruno's telling us the thief is Jack Dunn. If he spoke and said 'That's the guy who took your trainers,' it couldn't be plainer. It's like he's putting up a paw and pointing."

"You don't think he just likes the way Jack Dunn's trainers smell?" Amy said.

Jack Dunn had noticed the dog now. "Hey, look at the weird pooch with the thing over his eyes," he said. He bopped the top of Bruno's head. "Get lost, weird pooch. Quit licking around me."

"Don't you dare touch that dog," Amy yelled.

Jack stared across the empty arcade and grinned.

"Oh-oh, Croak," he said. "Look what the cat dragged in."

Croak turned his cap so that the peak was in the back. "That was no cat, that was an ugly old dog with a thing across its eyes," he said.

"He's part bloodhound," Amy said, "and he's blindfolded so nothing can distract him."

"What did she say?" Jack Dunn asked Croak.

Amy was talking funny, probably because she was holding her nose. She ran forward and whipped Mr Sabaton's red handkerchief off Bruno's eyes. "There, doggie!"

Bruno blinked twice and smiled up at Jack Dunn.

"And you, Jack Dunn." Colin pointed. "You give me back my trainers. I know you took them."

"Who? Me?" Jack Dunn smiled an innocent smile.

"Who? Us?" Croak smiled, too. He pointed at Colin's bare feet. "Aw, but look, Jack, he did lose his nice trainers."

Colin was so mad he could hardly breathe.

Bruno licked Jack Dunn's shoes, dribbling and making happy sounds.

"Must be those fish heads we rubbed on them, Jack," Croak said. "The mutt likes the way they taste."

"See?" Webster thumped the video machine and Spaceman flew forward a couple of centimetres. "You guys *were* cheating. We knew it. You're not supposed to rub anything on your trainers. The smell's supposed to happen naturally."

Jack Dunn bent down and shoved Bruno away. "Don't slobber on my shoes, mutt. I don't want those nice rotten-fish smells washed off." He looked up at Colin. "That was pretty dumb, losing your trainers like that. You shouldn't leave them outside your door. Me, now, I keep mine under lock and key when I'm not wearing them."

"You... you thief..." Colin began.

"I asked Poppy Roginski today in school if she was coming to the park to see me win tomorrow," Jack Dunn said.

"And what did she say?" Webster asked. "Drop dead?"

"Naw." Jack Dunn grinned. "She said she'd be there for sure."

"Maybe she'll even come to see us play today," Croak said. "She likes baseball."

Poppy Roginski had talked to Jack Dunn! Said words, whole sentences even. Colin took a deep breath. Then he leaned forward and grabbed a handful of Jack Dunn's jacket.

"Where did you hide my trainers, you dirty rotten..." His face was so close to Jack Dunn's that he could see the zits under his skin, almost ready to come out.

Webster pulled him back. "Come on, Col. We don't have any time to waste." He pushed Colin in front of him to the door.

Mr Sabaton and Amy dragged Bruno on his lead. Bruno did not want to leave.

"I don't think it's a good sign that Bruno likes Jack's shoes so much," Amy said. "They are pretty stinky. Maybe he will win after all."

"Colin's were worse," Webster said. "Bruno wouldn't even go near Colin's, that's how bad they were. Colin's were abominations. But what does it matter now? Colin's are gone."

Gone. Colin thought that was the saddest word he'd ever heard.

five

Colin and Webster and Amy and Mr Sabaton stood outside their block of flats. Bruno lay exhausted at Mr Sabaton's feet, recovering from his return trip across the street.

"I did warn you that Bruno was only part bloodhound," Mr Sabaton said. "I think he got carried away by the fish heads. I never give him treats like that."

"Bruno was excellent," Colin said. "He led us right to the thief. The thief just didn't have my trainers with him, that's all."

"We should call the police," Amy said.

"Police?" Webster asked. "They're not going to..." He stopped.

Across the street Jack Dunn and Croak swaggered out of the video arcade. Croak pointed at the group and Colin heard them laugh.

"They're going to play a baseball game and they don't even care about us," Amy said. She looked as if she might cry. Colin knew how she felt.

"Can we be certain they are the ones who took your trainers?" Mr Sabaton asked.

"Of course we can be certain," Colin said. "You heard Jack Dunn say that I shouldn't have left my trainers outside the door. He knew. He took them."

"Usually when a crime is committed, someone in the building is guilty," Mr Sabaton said.

"Like who?" Colin held up four fingers. "There's you and Mrs Knight upstairs. And Pam and George in flat two. Mrs Knight likes me a lot. I take her newspaper up to her so she won't have to go down to get it. I carry her groceries up for her. Pam and George are cool. They have their own great-looking trainers. Designer stuff. Why would they want mine?"

"A workman perhaps?" Mr Sabaton suggested.

"There was no workman," Colin said, "and you saw the way Jack and Croak looked at each other. You heard them laugh."

"I heard." Amy was stroking Bruno. Colin saw the hole in the side of her old trainer. She'd ripped it on the playground slide. Those trainers of hers would be lucky to last another week. Mum hadn't said anything, but Colin knew she was waiting to see if he'd win the three pairs before she spent money on new ones. He told himself it was Mum's fault that his trainers had been stolen. She had made him leave them outside. But he couldn't really blame her. They had stunk something awful. Even Amy's hamster had dropped, gasping, on the bottom of his cage when Colin had worn the trainers inside. He clenched his fists. They'd have won the competition for sure.

"Try to think what that boy might have done with them," Mr Sabaton suggested.

"Trashed them," Webster said.

Colin scowled. "Dumped them."

"He sure didn't keep them," Amy said.

"Well." Mr Sabaton looked at his watch. "It's almost four. Bruno and I like to watch *Love of Life*. If we can be of no further assistance...?"

"Not really. Thanks." Colin patted Bruno's head.

Amy scrambled up. "I'd better go in, too. It's time to wake Dad. I'm sorry, Col."

Colin blinked. "Me, too."

He and Webster watched them go inside. "Let's search the video arcade," Colin said.

"Wherever Jack Dunn dumped my trainers, he didn't have that much time."

They searched behind all of the machines. There were cobwebs and spiders and mice-nibbled candy wrappers. No trainers.

They searched the skip out the back. "Week-old doughnuts," Webster said. "We should take a couple for Bruno. I promised him all kinds of things."

They looked in every empty washing machine at the Launderette and in every empty dryer. They found a sock and a ten pence piece and three different-coloured buttons. But no trainers.

They checked behind the shrubbery in front of Colin's block of flats and in front of the building next door. They tried to be bloodhounds themselves, stopping every few steps to turn their heads and sniff. Nothing. Not even a whiff of a smell.

"I give up," Webster said. "Jack Dunn could have thrown them into a passing truck. Those trainers could be in New York by now."

"Wait," Colin said. A thought had slithered into his head. A great thought. "I know what we can do. We can take *his* trainers. We'll tell him we'll give them back when he gives back mine. We'll be able to bargain."

"Yeah!" Webster grinned. "But how are we going to get his trainers? He keeps them under lock and key when he's not wearing them. That's what he said."

"He's not wearing them when he's wearing his baseball boots," Colin said, "and there's no place with lockers at Jamison Park." He glanced up at the clock on the Willis Department Store. "It's four thirty. The Power-Up baseball game has started. What do you think, Webbie?"

Webster smiled through gritted teeth. "Play ball," he said.

six

Jamison Park was ten minutes away if you walked. Colin and Webster jogged.

They passed the famous dog-poop tree, and Webster gave Colin a look. "It could have been great," he said.

Cheering came from the wooden benches, which were half-filled with parents and relatives. They sat in two groups with space between them. On one side were the Power-Ups, on the other, the Lions.

Colin didn't really look for Poppy Roginski, but he couldn't help noticing that she wasn't there watching Jack Dunn. That cheered him up a little bit.

The Lions were batting, the Power-Ups fielding.

"There's Jack Dunn," Colin said. "Left field. And old Croak at third base."

He and Webster moseyed across to where a bunch of kids from their school were clumped between home base and first. Behind them to their left was the Power-Up dugout. Three guys were warming the bench. Rollie Burch and Vinnie and Francis Gomez. They jumped up when something was happening, then plopped back down again.

"Do you see Jack's trainers anywhere?" Webster whispered.

"Sure do." Colin spoke from one side of his mouth. "Under the bench. On their own.

Away from the others. Probably too stinky to be next to anyone else's."

"That's the sign of a good abomination," Webster said gloomily.

"It makes them easy to get to." Colin watched the game. "We have to plan this, Webbie. If we snatch those trainers at the right time, no one will see us."

The Lions batter hit a high fly.

There was a cheer from the stands.

The fielders went back, back, their faces turned to the sky.

The third baseman had spun around to watch the ball curve.

The three bench-warmers were on their feet.

"Now," Colin whispered.

He leaped down the steps into the dugout, scooped up the trainers and ran.

Webster ran beside him. They didn't stop till they passed the oak tree.

"If we're lucky, he won't miss them till the

game's over," Colin gasped. "Then I'll call him and say 'OK, let's trade.' "

"He'll probably call you or come in person," Webster warned. "Look out."

"That's OK, as long as he brings my abominations with him," Colin said.

He held Jack Dunn's trainers in front of him at arm's length. "Phew! Fish city." Now that the air wasn't rushing past his nose, he was getting the smell full force. "I've got to find somewhere good to hide them," he said. "These are the stinkiest..."

They were jogging through an alley behind Main Street. The alley wasn't one you'd hang around in, not if you didn't have to. It was littered with rubbish. Being barefoot, Colin watched where he ran. In here, he could step in things that were a lot worse than what was under the oak tree in Jamison Park.

A brick wall with a lot of broken spaces in it ran along the back of the alley. "Here," Colin said. "Give me a boost."

He stood on Webster's shoulders and slid the trainers into a gap in the bricks.

When he got down, they both stood back.

"Can you see them?" he asked Webster.

"Uh-uh." Webster shook his head. "Great spot."

Colin looked along the alley, imagining. It would be like one of those old Western movies. Jack Dunn would come along one way, holding out Colin's trainers. Colin would come the other way, holding Jack Dunn's. They'd meet. Gunfight at the OK Corral. Well, not really. More like a kidnap and exchange of ransom.

He felt great. He and Webster were back in business.

seven

Webster came to a stop at the corner of the next street.

"I gotta go home," he said. "My reading teacher comes at six. She says I'm doing great. I'll be able to read *War and Peace* pretty soon. I dunno, though. It looks hard to me."

Webster always jabbered when he was nervous and Colin could tell he was nervous now.

He paused, looked sideways at Colin, and said, "When are you going to call him?"

"About seven," Colin said. "He'll be home by then. I'll call you after and let you know what the set-up is."

Colin watched Webster go, then headed home. He dusted off the bottom of his feet with his hands before he went inside.

As soon as he opened their own door, he saw his dad standing by the stove. He was wearing his white apron that read "A man's work is never done" and stirring a big pot of spaghetti.

Amy was setting the table. She looked up as the door opened.

"Colin, oh, Colin." She dropped the forks. One of the green place mats went skipping off the table, the forks clattering along with it.

Amy ran towards him. "Something awful has happened."

Dad let the spaghetti he'd lifted on the spoon puddle back into the water.

"What?" Colin asked.

"We have your trainers," Amy said.

Colin stared at her. "You have my trainers?"

"Amy and I tried to find you to tell you," Dad said, "but you'd disappeared."

"We even called Webbie's," Amy added. "Where were you?"

"We went to the ball game for a while," Colin was stunned. He couldn't get past Amy's first unbelievable words. "You mean Jack Dunn brought my trainers back? Already?" he asked. He stopped. "What is it that's so awful about that?"

Amy took a bag from Colin's chair and thrust it into his hands. The trainers glowed white and ghostly through the plastic.

"What?" Colin's mind couldn't catch on to it. The trainers had new laces in them, ones with no frayed ends and no knots. "They've... they've been washed!" he gasped.

A card on a red cord dangled from the top of the bag. Colin pulled it off.

It said:

Dear Colin,

You're always so nice to me. There's so little I can do for you. I see your shoes outside all the time. I wish I could afford to buy you a new pair, but since I can't, I fixed these up. I used Shrink-No-More, which is guaranteed, so I hope they still fit. The laces are new.

Your friend,

Ella May Knight

P.S. The toe holes were too much for me.

"She didn't know about the competition," Amy said sadly. "She was paying you back for bringing in her papers and carrying her groceries and that time you went to the chemist for her."

"I know, I know." Colin took the shoes out of the bag. They smelled lemony fresh. He stuck his fingers through the toe holes.

"It's too bad, Col. I'm really sorry." Dad

wiped his hands on the front of his apron. He rubbed Colin's head, then hugged him tight. "But there's nothing you can do about it now, not a thing."

"Mum's bringing home apple pie from the little shop next to her office," Amy said. "It's to make you feel better."

Colin tried to smile. Usually he loved apple pie, but right now he didn't feel so good. He knew even apple pie wouldn't make him feel better.

eight

"It wasn't Jack Dunn and Croak after all," Arny said. "I'm really glad you didn't punch them out, Colin. You almost did."

"I know." Colin picked up the bag that held his trainers. "But Jack said I shouldn't have left them outside my door. That made me extra sure he'd taken them. How did he know?" He stopped and hit his head with his hand. "Oh, criminy, sure! Mrs H makes Jack Dunn and me sit by the open window in English class because of the smell."

"I guessed," Dad said, crinkling his eyes.

"And I said that was at least better than what my mum made me do. She made me leave my trainers outside the flat. I suppose... I guess maybe Jack Dunn heard. And then, when I said I'd lost them, he said..."

Dad nodded. "That's what must have happened."

Suddenly Colin thought about Jack Dunn. He pictured him coming off the field after the third or fourth inning, checking under the bench. No trainers. He'd freak out. Colin knew the feeling. And Jack would have to stay till the end of the game. He'd be dropping every fly ball to centre field.

"Why don't you go have a shower, Col," Dad said gently. "Mum will be home any minute."

Colin tried to think. If he could take Jack

Dunn's trainers back now, set them under the bench again... It would be a miracle.

"I think I have to go out for a while," he said.

Dad stopped halfway to the stove. "Uh-uh. It's getting dark. What's so important that you have to do it tonight?"

Colin swallowed. What if he told him?

"Maybe he's going up to Mrs Knight's. To thank her," Amy suggested.

Colin half nodded. That was an idea. He thought Amy must have been taking helpful lessons from Webbie.

"Why don't you call her instead?" Dad asked. "That would be just as good."

Colin hesitated. He didn't want to tell Dad the real reason.

He didn't want to tell him what he'd done. He could guess the kind of thing Dad would say. Stuff about right and wrong. And he'd be ashamed of Colin. Colin could almost hear him. *I wouldn't have believed you could ever do a mean thing like that.*

Dad was talking again. "Why don't you go have that shower, Colin, then you can call Mrs Knight. You'll feel better."

Colin nodded. He could think in the shower. He could decide what to do.

The hot water felt great. He scrubbed and scrubbed himself. His feet curled and cramped – they'd probably forgotten the feel of water. But then they remembered and he let them spread out and enjoy it.

Up at Jamison Park it would be the sixth or seventh inning now. Jack and Croak would have figured out what had happened. *Wait till we get that Colin Kyle. We'll massacre him.* Croak would grin that awful grin and smack one fist into the other the way he did. Man! Morbid!

He was drying off when he heard his mum come home, and he sat on the bathroom stool to put on his trainers. They were beaten-up but dazzling. Mrs Knight's Shrink-No-More had worked well. His toes were a bit jammed, but maybe they'd just expanded in the water.

He widened the toe holes with two fingers. By tomorrow they'd feel fine. Not that tomorrow mattered any more – not for him. For him it was just another day. He hung up the towel and went into the kitchen.

"Hi, hon." Mum glanced down at his trainers. "I'm so sorry, Colin." She came across quickly to hug him. "I know you wanted to win."

"To make Poppy Roginski like him," Amy butted in.

"Shush, Amy," Mum told her. "You wanted to get free shoes for you and Amy so that Dad and I wouldn't have to buy them. I can't say we wouldn't have been delighted, but it's not the end of the world." She held Colin a little away from her and smiled at him.

"Now, how about if you call Mrs Knight and thank her, then we'll eat. That spaghetti smells great."

"And I've made my special tofu and spinach sauce," Dad said.

Colin tried not to groan. As if life weren't bad enough.

He got Mrs Knight on the first ring. "It was a pleasure for me to do it, Colin," she said. "You and I are friends. Friends do nice things for each other."

"Yes," Colin said. "Thank you very much."

He went back to the kitchen and when his mum asked, "OK?" he nodded. Nothing was OK. But he couldn't tell her that.

He was halfway through the apple pie when the phone rang. He'd known it would and he'd figured out what to say. "It's for me," Colin said quickly. "Excuse me, please."

"Kyle?" The voice on the phone snarled like a hungry lion, but Colin knew who it was all right. He swallowed. "Who is this?"

"You know who it is. You'd better get my shoes back to me, pronto. I'm not kidding either. And don't try to tell me you didn't take them, because Vinnie and Francis Gomez saw you hanging around at the game."

"Listen," Colin said. "I did take them and I'm sorry. It was a mistake."

"You're right," the snarling voice said. "It was the biggest mistake of your life."

Colin hurried on. "But I have them in a safe place. I'm going to get them first thing in the morning. First thing... around dawn. And I'm going to bring them to you in time for the competition. I'll bring them right to the park."

"I want them now. I'm coming over."

Colin hunched his neck into his shoulders. Jack Dunn would. No question. He was the kind of guy who would walk right into another guy's flat. He might even bring his big, rotten, brother, Shrike. Colin made his voice calm, though it wasn't easy. "No use your coming now. I don't have the trainers. Where they are I can't get them till the morning, but they're safe." He listened to the silence. "Look," he added, "the competition's at ten. I'll be there. With your trainers. I promise it on the head of Kalamazoo."

Kalamazoo was their school's fat grey rabbit and mascot. A promise on Kalamazoo's head was sacred.

He listened to more silence. Jack Dunn must be thinking it over. Jack thought pretty slowly. "You don't have any choice," Colin said to help him along. "You have to trust me."

"Be there," Jack Dunn said at last. "And my trainers better smell just as good as when you stole them. You got that, Colin Kyle?"

"Got it," Colin said.

nine

The phone rang again at about eight o'clock.

"For you, Colin," Mum called.

Webbie! Colin thought. I forgot to call Webbie.

But it wasn't Webbie, it was Jack Dunn's big brother, Shrike.

"You know who I am?" he asked Colin.

"Yes," Colin breathed. "You are Jack Dunn's big brother, Shrike."

"I know who you are, too. Don't forget that." Shrike banged down the phone.

Colin put his hand on his chest. His heart leaped like a frog in a jumping competition. He had to lean against the wall, waiting for it to slow down, before he called Webster.

Webster was stunned when he heard about Mrs Knight washing Colin's trainers.

"Are they awful now? All clean and everything?" he asked.

"Like brand new, except for the holes in the toes," Colin said.

"But, oh, criminy! What about Jack Dunn's trainers...?" Webster began.

"Jack Dunn called," Colin said. "And don't faint yet. Shrike the Terrible called, too."

He thought he heard Webster give a little whimper.

"So we have to get up early and go get those trainers off the wall and take them to the park," Colin said. "I promised. And not only that, our lives are at stake."

There was total silence on the other end of the line.

"Webbie? Are you still there?"

"Will Shrike the Terrible be with his brother when we give the trainers back?" Webster asked.

"Yes," Colin said.

Webster groaned. "We're doomed."

"We're doomed if we don't," Colin said. "Meet me at seven in the morning on our front steps. I need a boost to reach the shoes."

"I don't see why the two of us have to go," Webster said. "Couldn't you drag over one of those rubbish bins and stand on it?"

"No," Colin said.

"It's just that we have pancakes for breakfast on Saturday mornings..." Webster began.

"It's just that I don't want to die alone," Colin said, and hung up. He knew Webbie would be there. He'd whine and complain, but he'd be there.

His mum and dad and Amy were watching TV in the living room. They asked him what programme he wanted to see. Amy said it was his turn to have *Star Trek*, though they both knew it was her turn to watch Nickelodeon.

"Thanks, Am," he said. He wished they weren't being so nice to him. It made things even harder.

Mum gave him the last helping of pie to take to bed. Colin thought about not taking it for self-punishment. But that didn't seem to make much sense, so he took it.

"You're still going to the competition tomorrow, aren't you, Col?" Mum asked.

Colin nodded. Tomorrow! Awful, hideous thought. He and Webbie would hand over Jack's trainers. Then Shrike would strike. No way would he forgive and forget.

"Colin will go watch the competition for sure," Amy said. "He won't want to miss seeing Poppy Roginski."

Colin decided Amy could never stay sweet for long. It wore off fast.

"He's going because he's a good sport, right, Col?" Mum said.

Colin nodded half-heartedly, not looking at her.

"Atta boy!" Dad said, and Colin gave him a bogus grin.

"I'm going to the park early, Mum," he said. "Probably before you and Dad are up. I want to check what's going on."

Dad smiled. "OK, son. Your mum and Amy and I will be there later. We like our Saturday morning sleep-in."

"Look out for us." Mum touched Colin's cheek. "And don't feel too bad. There'll be another competition next year. You can get in training for it right away."

"Yuk. Spare us," Amy said. "Can't we have a breathing space?"

Yep. Her sweetness wore off fast, all right. Not that Colin cared. Things weren't going to be so sweet for him from now on, anyway.

ten

Colin set his alarm for five minutes to seven.
Which wasn't quite dawn, but close.

In the morning he shut off the bell as soon
as it rang, but he wasn't fast enough. Just as
he was tiptoeing to the bathroom, Amy came
out of her room.

She yawned. "What's up? It's only seven.
You're going now?"

"Yup. And I'm in a hurry."

"I want to come, too." Amy was talking baby-speak, the way she did when she wanted her own way.

She waited by the bathroom door, then followed Colin back to his room. "How come you're in such a hurry?"

"Get lost," Colin said. "I have to get dressed."

She sat on the edge of his bed. "It's about your trainers, isn't it? You and Webbie are going to muck them up in some way. You're going to the oak tree after all."

"Will you just disappear?" Colin said.

"I'm getting dressed, too, and I'm going to follow you," Amy announced. "So you might as well tell. I'll find out anyway."

Colin sighed. "You're such a pain, Amy," he said. "OK."

He told her while they quickly ate bowls of cereal and while Colin wrote a note and taped it to the fridge. *Amy came with me. See you at the park.*

"Oh, boy! Do you think Shrike the Terrible will be there for sure?" Amy asked. "I've never seen him. Jennifer Hyatt's big sister says he's the worst boy in the whole high school. He beats up kids all the time. Once he closed a locker on a Year Five girl's hair and left her. *Left* her. She could have died of starvation."

"Thanks a lot for telling me all this," Colin said. "I feel better now."

They went quietly along the corridor and then outside. A mockingbird called hello from an elm tree. A cat slid slyly from behind a bush. Colin saw Webster puffing along. His T-shirt was inside out and back to front, the tag sticking out under his chin. His hair was spiked up like a scrubbing brush.

Colin was wearing his best blue knitted shirt with the alligator on the pocket. He hoped it wouldn't get bloodied. But Poppy Roginski would be at the contest, and the shirt made his eyes look bluer. That's what his Aunt Noni had told him once.

"How come Amy's here?" Webster asked as soon as he got to them.

Amy said with a sniff, "Because I'm Colin's sister, and I've been in on this since the beginning. That's why."

Webster looked down at Colin's shoes. "Man," he said. "Disaster. How come that lady didn't mind her own business?"

"How come you don't mind yours?" Colin said angrily. "Don't talk. Just come."

Webster shrugged. "Well, let's go get Jack Dunn's shoes quick," he said. "Then I can go home. You won't need me just to give them back. I can eat breakfast and be there later."

"When Shrike has worn himself out beating me up?" Colin finished. "I thought a manager was supposed to stick with you, win or lose. Live or die."

"OK, OK. It was just a try," Webster said. "Let's go."

There was hardly any traffic this early on a Saturday morning. Colin thought even Bruno could have crossed the street, no problem. First sun, warm and comforting, dropped white on the pavement. But the alley was cold, the light still hidden behind the buildings.

Amy looked around nervously. "Where did you put the trainers, anyway?"

"Don't worry," Webster said. "We know just where to find them."

Colin slowed. "Does the alley look different to you, Webbie? Cleaner or something?"

Webster turned in a slow circle. "It is cleaner. And look at the big puddles of water. It's been hosed down. The cardboard boxes are gone."

Colin took another step. "Oh, no," he said, and then he was running, Webster behind him, Amy behind Webster.

"There's the piece of broken wall." Colin stood on tiptoe, then began kangaroo-jumping in front of the gap. He couldn't even see the grey back edge of a grungy trainer.

"Quick, Webbie!"

Webster bent over, touching his toes. Colin put a foot on his back, then stood. The gap in the wall was empty. "They're gone," he said. "Jack Dunn's trainers are gone!"

eleven

"Hey, you." A guy in a white apron was sweeping the alley in the back of the pizza shop.

Colin jumped down from Webster's back.

"Are you looking for those nasty trainers that were on the wall?" the guy asked.

Hope exploded in Colin, leaving him breathless.

"Have you got them?" Amy asked.

"Heck, no." The guy leaned on the broom. "Who'd touch those grisly things? Except Pete, of course. He's the fellow who cleans up here every Saturday morning early, before the rubbish truck comes. Washes the place down."

"What did he do with them?" Colin asked.

"Chucked them away with the rubbish, of course. Sometimes he keeps stuff he finds. Once he got a really nice radio someone left behind, and once—"

"Where's the rubbish?" Colin wondered if something was happening to his hearing. His head was filled with a booming sound, but maybe it was just his frightened earlobes fluttering.

"Oh, the rubbish truck came and left about an hour ago. You didn't want those trainers, did you?"

"Certainly not." Webster hit the brick wall with his hand. "Those were just our insurance policies against instant death, that's all. Those were our *parachutes*. You've heard of Shrike the Terrible?"

The guy had stopped sweeping again. His nose lifted as if he could smell disaster. "*Who* the Terrible?" he asked eagerly.

Colin took a deep, shaky breath. "Where does the rubbish truck go from here?"

"Down Main Street. Picking up as it goes. Sometimes you can hear it for a while, banging and rattling about." He cocked his head. "Listen. Hear it? It's probably only a few streets away."

"Oh, thank you, thank you, thank you." Colin waved frantically at Webster and Amy. "Come on. We might get to it before it goes to the dump."

"The refuse collector's name's Hubbel," the pizza guy called. "His buddy's Eddie. He's a little guy. Tell them you know me."

Webster panted along beside Colin. "Now wait a sec. We're going to search a rubbish truck? Oh, man. Do you know what kind of stuff's in a rubbish truck?"

"Don't talk. Run," Colin commanded.

"Maybe there's a radio," Amy said, puffing along. "The kind the alley guy found."

"Some chance." Webster's untied shoelaces danced a jig at every step. "There'll be old, chewed hamburgers, potato peelings, squashed tomatoes..." He was out of breath but struggled on. "Flies. Ants by the million."

Colin could hear the loud *thump, thump* of a heavy motor only about one street away. Metal banged against metal. He looked back at Webster. "Do you want to face Jack Dunn and Shrike the Terrible, or do you want to face a million little harmless ants?"

"I love ants," Webster said.

Colin stopped and held up a hand. "Listen. Do you think they're on the next street or the one after that? We have no time to waste. If they fill up, they'll head for the dump and we're dead."

"Boys! Amy!" Someone was calling to them from across the street. They turned.

It was Mr Sabaton with Bruno on the lead, out for their morning round-and-round-the-block-again walk.

"Bruno!" Colin breathed. "I bet he could help us find those shoes."

"He loved those shoes," Amy said. "I bet he could find them in a mountain of rubbish. What a great idea, Col."

The three of them raced across the street.

"A rubbish truck?" Mr Sabaton said when they told him. "I don't know if Bruno—"

"Oh, please, Mr Sabaton," Amy begged. "It could help save Colin's life."

"Mine, too, in case you've forgotten," Webster said sarcastically.

"Webbie's, too."

"What do you say, Bruno?"

"Woof." Bruno's nose was down and at the ready.

"He'll have to be carried across the street, remember," Mr Sabaton warned.

"No problem," Colin said. Bruno lay down, made himself limp, and closed his eyes.

"Good doggie," Amy said. "He's on."

twelve

They decided not to blindfold Bruno. There were fewer distractions at this time of the morning.

"Hurry!" Colin called as he saw the tail end of the rubbish truck disappearing around the corner into the next street.

Bruno strained at the lead.

"You take him," Mr Sabaton said. "The pace is too much for me."

Bruno pulled so hard he gagged and slobbered. "OK, boy, don't kill yourself," Colin pleaded.

There ahead of them was the truck, parked in the Pure Food Market car park.

Hubbel and the kid, Eddie, were tipping the contents of a big rubbish bin into the truck's open back.

Colin panted up beside them. They both glanced down at Bruno and moved quickly out of the lead's reach.

"We're friends of the pizza guy," Colin said.

"You mean Warren?" Hubbel asked.

"I suppose so." Colin reeled Bruno in tighter so that he wouldn't have to shout at Hubbel and Eddie. "We accidentally left a pair of trainers in the alley. They accidentally got thrown into the truck. Could we jump in and see if we can find them?"

Hubbel narrowed his eyes. "You want to look through my rubbish?"

"We're not going to steal any of it,"

Webster offered, helpful to the end.

"Hey!" Eddie wiped his gloved hand across his nose. "I remember those trainers. They're about halfway back, in the middle of the heap."

Webster groaned.

Amy petted Bruno, who lay with his head between his paws, his ears as flat as a bulldog's ears can get. "Remember the fish-head trainers, Bruno?" she cooed. "Remember how much you loved them? Go and dig for them. We'll lift you up. Find them, boy."

Bruno's tail wagged in a depressed sort of way.

"Wait just a second here," Hubbel said. "You're proposing that a dog dig through my rubbish? That's not permitted. Never."

Bruno sighed happily.

"Oh, please, Mr Hubbel," Amy begged. "Please. It truly is life or death for us."

Hubbel's gloved hand stroked his chin. He closed his eyes. "Oh, all right, little lady. But he has to keep it tidy. We have a system. Our rubbish is layered. No messing it about."

"Thanks a lot," Colin said. He couldn't figure out why grown-ups couldn't resist Amy. He could certainly resist her.

He and Webster gathered up Bruno and began to lift him into the back of the truck. "Whoa! Whoa! Easy!" Webster muttered as Bruno scrabbled and pushed against them. His bowed back legs pounded at Colin's chest. He doggy-paddled in the air. They set him down and he collapsed in a quaking mass of fur.

Amy groaned. "Oh, no. He's fainted."

"Fake faint," Webster said. "This dog has problems."

Mr Sabaton, out of breath, quickly came up beside them.

"Good," Colin said. "Bruno will be happier with you around."

Mr Sabaton knelt beside his dog and stroked his quivering head. "I neglected to tell you," he said. "Bruno does not like to get his paws dirty. He's very fastidious."

"Fast what?" Webster asked.

"Fastidious. That means he likes to keep his paws clean."

Colin began to climb up on to the truck bed. "Come on, Webbie," he said, "get a move on."

"I'm very fastidious myself," Webster began. "I could direct from here. Managers—"

"Get up here," Colin said, "and get up now."

Webster sighed. "How come you listen to a dog and not to me?" he began.

But Colin was already in the truck and was hauling Webster up behind him.

thirteen

"You're not leaving me behind," Amy said. "Give me a hand, Webbie."

"Amy," Colin said. "Mum would kill me. Think of the germs."

"Five minutes," Hubbel called. "That's all the time I can give you. This truck has to roll."

"Pull her up, Webbie," Colin said. "We need all the help we can get."

"You will excuse me," Mr Sabaton said. "I don't think I could quite manage it."

"He's probably fastidious," Webster whispered.

"It's perfectly all right, Mr Sabaton," Colin said.

He and Webster and Amy waded knee-deep into the rubbish.

Hubbel closed one eye, ran a thumb in the air measuring distance and space. "Say one-third of the way back and second layer down. That should do it. Forward a little. Right now you're in the shopping-centre section."

"You want our gloves?" Eddie asked. They tossed them up and Eddie found a spare pair in the truck for Amy. The gloves were so big they could have been baseball mitts.

"Thanks," Amy said.

And then they were digging, puddling through the mess. It felt just like wading in wet oatmeal. And why was it warm through his jeans? Colin wondered. Warm, and wet, and steamy.

"Keep it neat, keep it neat," Hubbel yelled. "We're responsible. That's our rubbish."

Webster wrinkled his nose. "He can have it!"

They scooped up mouldy oranges, black bananas that squelched up out of their skins, wizened cabbages.

"The produce market," Eddie called.

"Should have been recycled," Mr Sabaton said severely. "Good compost."

The smell was terrible. Flies buzzed around their heads. Ants crawled up their gloves and over their arms.

Amy shuddered. "Yuck. I just stepped on something soft and slimy."

"Don't look at it," Webster advised.

"Three minutes," Hubbel called, checking his watch. He and Eddie sat on the back ramp of the Pure Food Market, drinking Diet Cokes.

Eddie raised his hand. "Happy searching."

"Sure," Webster muttered.

They found chicken bones and meat bones and bones that could have been from a tyrannosaurus rex.

Webster gasped. "I think I'm going to throw up."

Eddie leaped to his feet. "Not on our rubbish, you're not. Lean over the stern."

"Wait! Look!" Colin hooted with joy. He hefted up an empty carton that had once held Fuji film. "Isn't there a Fuji shop that backs on to the alley?"

"Sure is, boy," Eddie said.

And at that minute Colin saw a shoelace, like a dirty, stringy worm. He burrowed deeper. "Yeah!" he yelled, holding up a fish-head trainer. He ducked back down and came up with the other one.

"Yeah!" His little hop of joy made a rotten tomato squirt under his foot. "We're saved, Webbie," he called. "Or partly saved."

"We may die, anyway," Webster said. "We're contaminated for life."

"Put everything back the way you found it," Hubbel consulted his watch again. "You have one minute." He pointed at Webster. "No, no, no! Don't mix the shopping-centre layer with the next-street layer."

Webster rolled his eyes.

When they were finished, the three of them stood beside Mr Sabaton and Bruno examining one another. Colin picked dried spaghetti from Amy's hair, but the sauce had stuck. Webster's inside-out T-shirt had an interesting black-and-slime-green design across the front.

"Don't change it right side out," Amy advised.

Colin held the trainers at arm's length, one in each hand.

Bruno gave them a halfhearted sniff, then lay down again.

"I hope he's OK," Amy said.

"He's just feeling that he let you down, that's all," Mr Sabaton said. "He'll be all right."

"Nasty smell from those trainers," Hubbel said. "Cod fish. I have a very educated nose."

"I'm sure," Webster said.

"Thanks a lot," Colin told Hubbel and Eddie. They gave back the gloves.

"We'd offer to wash them," Amy said, "but—"

"Wash our gloves?" Hubbel and Eddie laughed as if that was pretty funny. "Let's go."

They climbed into the truck cab and clattered away, waving through the open windows.

Webster stood with his legs apart and his arms held out to the sides. "I'm the Swamp Monster," he told Amy.

"Yeah, well, I'm the Slime Queen," she said. She nodded at Colin. "And that's my brother, the Scum Bag."

"So first we go home and shower and then we take the fish-head trainers to the park."

Colin shook his head. "No time. Straight to the park."

"Like this?" Amy squeaked. "Mum will have a fit."

"Like this," Colin said.

Webster looked at Amy. "So much for being fastidious," he said.

fourteen

The Swamp Monster, the Queen of Slime, and the Scum Bag raced past the clock on the Willis Department Store.

"Oh, no! It's ten already," Colin called back over his shoulder. "Jack Dunn is going to be raging like an angry bull."

"Not to mention Croak – and Shrike. Three angry bulls." Webster slowed. "Wait, Colin.

Maybe we shouldn't go. What's the good if we're too late? We could buy one-way tickets to the Malaysian jungle and build a treehouse."

Colin ran on. Amy passed Webster and Webster shrugged his shoulders and tagged along, too. He kept talking as he ran. "Anyway, Jack Dunn is just a big cheat. *Fish-head* trainers! He doesn't deserve to win."

They were at the park. In the distance Colin saw the masses of people standing around and the long line of contestants. In front of them were three figures at a table. He decided they were the judges. All of the people seemed to be staring across the field at them. Colin stopped, and Amy and Webster crowded into him.

"I think I'm in extreme shock," Webster muttered. "Look." Running towards them was Jack Dunn, Croak, and Shrike the Terrible, the biggest of the three, big as a giant.

Webster moved so that he was all the way behind Colin.

"Colin," Amy said. "Mum and Dad are over in the stands. I see them. Shrike the Terrible can't do anything to us when our parents and all those people are right there – can he?" Her voice trailed off.

Colin held up the trainers, one in each hand. Once in a movie he'd seen the hero hold things out like that to calm the evil monster.

"We have them. We brought them." The shaky voice was Webster's, coming from behind Colin. Just the voice came, not Webster himself.

"About time," Jack Dunn grabbed the trainers from Colin's hands. He dropped them on to the grass and began pulling off his hard black shoes.

"Where were you guys? Down in the sewers?" Croak asked. He stuck one of his fingers down his throat and rolled his eyes.

"We weren't in a flower garden," Colin said.

"Well, we couldn't have held this competition back one more minute, you creeps," Jack Dunn said. "I could have lost out all because of you."

"Wait." It was the first word Shrike had spoken, a snarl of a word. "Let me smell those trainers. If you guys have de-stunk them, you'll never live to see another day."

"We didn't de-stink them," Webster whined. "We didn't, honest, sir. They're even better now."

Shrike sniffed a deep, close-up sniff. Anyone else would have passed out, but Shrike was made of stronger stuff. "They're OK," he said. "We'll use the bottle, anyway. Croak! Stand between me and the rest of the people."

Croak arranged himself to block all views. Shrike took a small glass bottle from his pocket. It said Vanilla Essence on the label, but when he unstoppered it, it was pretty clear that it was not vanilla essence.

Colin's eyes watered. His nose burned. He grabbed at his throat.

Shrike poured some drops on each trainer. "The finishing touch," he said, grinning at Colin.

"Omigosh!" Amy stepped back and held her nose. "What is it?" A blackbird that had been resting on the grass took off with a squawk, its feathers fluffed up.

From across the field came a voice through a megaphone. "Mr Jack Dunn, are you ready?"

"Coming," Croak croaked.

Colin tried not to breathe, then asked, "What is it?"

"I made it in the lab," Shrike said. "Not that you dumbos would know what I'm talking about. It's hydrogen sulphide."

"It smells like eggs that have rotted for ten hundred million years," Webster said.

"You're cheating again," Amy said. "You're nothing but awful, miserable cheats."

"The thing is, you don't even have to cheat," Colin said. "These trainers of yours are the foulest—"

"You're sure this stuff won't burn?" Jack Dunn asked, ignoring Colin and jamming his feet into the damp trainers.

"Nah," Shrike said. "You'll knock 'em dead, that's all. Remember, one of those winning pairs goes to me. I wear a size thirteen."

"It figures," Webster muttered, low enough so nobody would hear him.

"Gentlemen! Gentlemen!" came the megaphone voice. "We must start the contest without you if you're not here immediately."

Jack Dunn tied his laces and stood up.

As he and Croak and Shrike the Terrible ran across the field, the revolting smell of eggs that had rotted for ten hundred million years lingered behind them.

fifteen

Colin's mum and dad came running to meet them. "What happened? Look at you!"

"It's a long story," Colin said. "We took Jack Dunn's trainers because we thought he'd taken mine. We were going to swap. But then we discovered he hadn't and..."

Colin stared down at himself. His blue knitted shirt with the alligator on the pocket that his Aunt Noni had said made his eyes look bluer had turned a strange, blotchy purple. The warm air and the running had dried his jeans. Now they were coated with scum like the skin on a parched mud puddle. He bent his knee and the scum cracked, little pieces dropping off.

"Then Jack's trainers accidentally got dumped in the rubbish," Webster butted in.

"So we got into the rubbish truck and searched," Amy added.

Mum shuddered. "You got into..." She picked a dried-up seed off Colin's arm. "You're peppered with these things. What are they?"

"Squashed tomato," Colin said, and Mum shuddered again.

"We knew if we didn't find the trainers Shrike the Terrible would massacre us," Webster explained.

"Yes, but it wasn't only that," Colin muttered.

Webster stared. "It wasn't? What was it?"

"Oh," Colin said vaguely. "He didn't take my trainers. That was the only reason I took his, so in the end it wasn't fair." He was looking over Webster's head at the people in the stands. Poppy Roginski wasn't there. He was sure of that. For some reason he could spot Poppy Roginski anywhere. It was like being able to pick out the North Star from among all the millions of other stars in the sky. Just as well she isn't here, he thought. I'm not exactly looking my best. But he was disappointed, too. He was always disappointed not to see Poppy Roginski.

His dad squeezed his shoulder. "I'm glad you got them back, Colin."

Across the field one of the judges was calling through the megaphone. "First contestant, take off your trainers. Bring them here and set them on the judges' table."

A boy with a big number one on his T-shirt put his trainers on the table and stepped back.

Colin was checking out the rest of the contestants. Some he knew from school. Number four he'd never seen before, and number five! Number five was Poppy Roginski. She was wearing pink shorts and a pink-and-white-striped top. Her black hair was held back with a pink-and-white-polka-dotted hairband. Colin thought she was as pretty as an Easter egg. On her feet were the nastiest-looking trainers he'd ever seen in his life. Maybe they'd been white once. Now they were a mouldering, festering, disgusting black.

Vaguely Colin heard his mother ask, "Would you and Amy like to go straight home and have a bath? Webbie, you, too?"

"I'd like to stay and watch the contest," Colin said.

"You've got to be kidding..." Webster began. And then he said, "Oh-oh. Look who's number five. It's Poppy Roginski!"

"Now I see why we've got to stay for the competition," Amy added.

The five of them walked across the grass. There were two men judges, one bald, one with a moustache. The other judge was a woman wearing a Mickey Mouse sweatshirt. Another man stood a little apart from the other three. He was dressed in a three-piece suit, waistcoat and all.

"Number five," the woman judge called out.

Poppy lifted her feet free of her unlaced abominations and carried her trainers up to the table.

The woman judge leaned towards her, then wafted a piece of paper across her own face as if she needed air.

"Our young lady contestant here says she wears her trainers when she's mucking out her duck house on their farm," she called to the audience. "And I certainly believe her."

There was a ripple of laughter from the crowd as Poppy put her trainers on the table and the two other judges pretended to faint.

That was when Poppy Roginski looked up and smiled at Colin. Smiled right at him. She was wearing her special-occasion pink braces on her teeth and her cheeks were pink, too. She was dazzling.

Colin thought he might faint himself.

sixteen

"I see Bruno and Mr Sabaton," Amy said, and she crouched down and called, "Bruno! Bruno, come!"

He came, furiously pulling Mr Sabaton across the grass.

"Look! It's Jack Dunn's turn," Mum said.

Number eleven was strutting to the table where the other pairs of stinky trainers sat in a numbered row. Each time the breeze wafted in their direction Colin could smell the blend of them. It was like the time a rat had died in the basement of their building. They hadn't found it for six days. When anyone had opened the basement door, phe-ew!

Jack Dunn set his trainers on the end of the table and the bald-headed judge propped the number eleven behind them.

"My word!" The judge whipped out a large white handkerchief and held it to his nose. "Are those rotten eggs I smell?"

Jack Dunn smiled. "No, those are my trainers."

The judge with the moustache gave them a cautious sniff. "A wonderful odour of decay," he said.

"He's going to win," Webster whispered glumly.

The woman judge poked the trainers with her pencil, then lifted one with the pencil point and examined it, but not too closely.

"Why the smell of rotten eggs?"

"Well, you see, ma'am, I live on a farm. It's my job to go out to the hen house and gather the eggs for my mother. Sometimes I accidentally stand on one or two."

Colin rolled his eyes.

"Jack Dunn lives in the town," he whispered to his dad.

"Isn't that a fish smell, too?" the woman judge asked.

"Yes, ma'am. A river runs through our back field. Sometimes fish jump out, you know? Flying fish? And we don't see them. That's why my trainers smell so great," Jack finished. "All natural."

"What a liar," Webster said.

"What a prat," Amy added.

The moustached judge had the megaphone now. "Well, number eleven is our final contestant. We'll take a few minutes now to make our very difficult decision."

Music suddenly blared from a loudspeaker

as Jack Dunn strutted back to his place in the line.

"Let's jump on him," Webster suggested. "Let's make him eat his rotten, cheating trainers. You and Amy could do it. I could be the lookout in case Shrike the Terrible tries to—"

"It's going to be a close call," Colin's dad said, and Colin's mum leaned across and whispered, "We're proud of you, Colin, for what you did."

Colin smiled at her. Yeah, he thought, but no new trainers for us. It was as if his mum read his thoughts. She could do that sometimes. "You wanted to win for us as much as for yourself. But as far as we're concerned, you're a winner now."

"Hear, hear," Mr Sabaton said. He unhooked the lead and Bruno found another dog running free and played tag with it around the oak tree.

Colin secretly watched Jack Dunn sneak up

behind Poppy Roginski and pull off her pink-and-white-polka-dotted hairband. He watched Poppy plead with him to give it back. Jack Dunn put the band on his own greasy hair, low on his forehead as if he was a surfer or a tennis player. As if he was the stinky-trainer king already.

The music stopped as abruptly as it had started and the woman judge took the megaphone. "This has been a tough decision," she said. "We have perfect examples of offensiveness here. One pair of trainers is just about as foul as the next. But it is the unanimous decision of the judges that number five, Miss Poppy Roginski, is the winner."

"Yeah! Super!" Everyone was applauding.

Webster grabbed Colin's arm. "This is great. Poppy likes us. Who needs three pairs of trainers? Maybe she'll give you a pair and me a pair and—"

"Dream on, Webster," Colin's dad said.

"Mr Dunker, owner of the Slam Dunker Stores and sponsor of this competition, will award the prize," the woman judge shouted.

The man in the three-piece suit walked across the grass during the cheering, took Poppy's hand, and escorted her to the table.

Colin thought Mr Dunker was the luckiest guy on earth. He thought Poppy Roginski was just like a beauty queen getting her crown, except that Poppy Roginski was prettier and smaller.

Jack Dunn sat on the grass wiggling his toes. He'd thrown Poppy Roginski's pink-and-white-polka-dotted hairband on the grass in front of him.

Cameras flashed and the crowd cheered as Poppy accepted the gift certificate and went back in line with the rest of the contestants.

"She just got it 'cause she's a girl and she's cute," Jack Dunn yelled.

Colin could hardly believe it.

"Boo," the crowd yelled. "Boo, bad sport."

And Colin couldn't believe what he was doing himself, either. He must have left his brains behind in the rubbish truck. He was hurrying over to Jack Dunn as fast as his stiff-legged jeans would let him walk.

Jack Dunn looked up when Colin stopped in front of him.

"You just shut up, Jack Dunn," Colin said. "Poppy Roginski won fair and square. You didn't, and that was fair and square, too."

"You little weasel," Jack Dunn said.

"Weasel yourself," Colin told him. "You and I will have another chance next year and, so help me, if you try any of that fish-and-egg-stuff again, I'll make you eat your cheating trainers."

Jack Dunn stood up. "Oh, yeah? You and who?"

"Me and my sister, Amy. Webster will be the lookout in case Shrike the Terrible comes by." Colin's knees were knocking and he was glad he had the stiff-legged jeans to hold him upright. He turned and picked up Poppy Roginski's pink-and-white-polka-dotted hairband. Dirt droplets dropped from him as his jeans cracked.

"Here," he told her. "Congratulations."

"Thank you." Poppy Roginski smiled her very attractive, pink-plastic smile.

"You're welcome," Colin said. He decided this was much better than winning the trainers. As he walked back towards his family, he counted the words over the loud beating of his heart. He'd said four to her. She'd said two to him.

It was a whole new beginning.